NOT LITTLE

Maya Myers

Pictures by Hyewon Yum

NEAL PORTER BOOKS

HOLIDAY HOUSE / NEW YORK

Neal Porter Books

Text copyright © 2021 by Maya Myers

Illustrations copyright © 2021 by Hyewon Yum

All Rights Reserved

HOLIDAY HOUSE is registered in the U.S. Patent and Trademark Office.

Printed and bound in March 2021 at C & C Offset, Shenzhen, China.

The artwork for this book was created with colored pencils.

Book design by Jennifer Browne

www.holidayhouse.com

First Edition

1   3   5   7   9   10   8   6   4   2

Library of Congress Cataloging-in-Publication Data

Names: Myers, Maya, author. | Yum, Hyewon, illustrator.

Title: Not little / by Maya Myers; illustrated by Hyewon Yum.

Description: First edition. | New York : Holiday House, 2021. | "A Neal
Porter Book." | Audience: Ages 3 to 7. | Audience: Grades K–1. |
Summary: Dot proves she is not little by standing up to a school bully.

Identifiers: LCCN 2020034173 | ISBN 9780823446193 (hardcover)

Subjects: CYAC: Size—Fiction. | Bullying—Fiction.

Classification: LCC PZ7.1.M9324 No 2021 | DDC [E]—dc23

LC record available at https://lccn.loc.gov/2020034173

ISBN 978-0-8234-4619-3

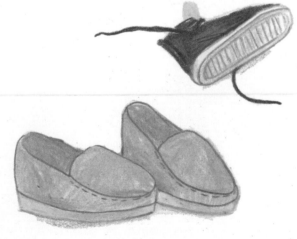

For my mom, small but mighty
and never afraid to use her voice. —M.M.

For Sahn, who has the biggest personality
even though he's the smallest in our family. —H.Y.

I am the smallest person in my family.

Even my name is small: Dot.

Everybody thinks
I am too little to do things.

Everybody is wrong.

I can do all kinds of things.

I may be small,
but I'm not little.

I am the smallest person
in my class, too.
People look at me
and ask if I'm
in preschool.

Then I tell them that the square root
of sixty-four is eight,
or that Jakarta is the capital of Indonesia,
or that my favorite Mars rover is *Curiosity*.

I'm not little.

At the library, they ask if I'm sure I want to check out such hard books.

At restaurants, they laugh when I order from the grown-up menu.

At the grocery store, they ask my mom, "Would your little girl like a sticker?"

I'm not little!

Today, there is a new boy in my class. His name is Sam.
He is very small.
He might even be smaller than I am.

I keep trying to get next to him so I can measure.

He doesn't say anything.

I wonder if he's afraid of me.

There is a mean boy at recess.
I always stay far away from him.
I see the mean boy talking to Sam.

I have a feeling he's saying
something not nice.

I decide I will sit next to Sam at lunch
to warn him about the mean boy.
Also to see if I am maybe taller than he is.

In the cafeteria, I see the mean boy
coming right toward us.
I freeze.

The mean boy stops next to Sam.

"Ew, gross. What *is* that, little baby?"
He says it very quietly, so no grown-ups can hear.

Sam hunches forward, getting even smaller.
I don't know what to do.

"Oh, I get it," says the mean boy. "That must be *baby* food."
Sam slumps lower.

I feel my heart beating very hard.
I take a deep breath.

"Hey," I say.
"That's mean."

The mean boy shoots his mean eyes at me. He snorts.
"What are *you* gonna do about it, little girl?"

Oh, man. Ohmanohmanohman.

The whole cafeteria is quiet,
like I hit the mute button.

The lunch lady
is looking at me.

The teacher
is looking at me.

The kids are
looking at me.

Sam is
looking at me.

And the mean boy is looking at me.

I don't move.
Nobody moves.

Then the teacher starts coming toward us,
and all the kids start looking around
and whispering to each other.

The teacher looks at the mean boy,
who is walking away fast.
She looks at me.

"Why don't you sit
down now, Dot?"
she says.

I sit down. I put my lunchbox down hard on the table.
My cheeks feel hot, and I blow hot breath out my nose.

"I'm not little,"
I say to no one.

"Dot?"
My name sounds even smaller
coming out of Sam's mouth.

I turn and look at him.

"I think . . ."

He chews on his lip and pushes up his glasses.
"I think you're the biggest kid I ever met."

"Ha!"

I say. But Sam isn't laughing.

"Oh!"

I say.

"Huh,"

I say.

Sam smiles.

I smile back.

And I stretch up a little straighter to see
if my nose is a little higher than his.

"Yeah, you're taller than me."
He shrugs. "Everybody is."

I unstretch, so our noses are the same height.
"Maybe," I say.

"But just a little."